Copyright © 2020 WAMAN BOOKS PUBLISHING, LLC

All rights reserved. No part of this publication may be used or reproduced in any manner whatsoever without written permission of the publisher.

Author: Reena Korde Pagnoni
Illustrator: Frances Rose Español
Editor: Lor Bingham, Calico Editing

ISBN: 978-1-7354613-4-2 (Paperback)

Library of Congress Control Number: 2020917356

— WB —
WAMAN BOOKS

Published by:
WAMAN BOOKS PUBLISHING, LLC
WWW.WAMANBOOKS.COM

THE RAMBEE BOO SERIES
RAMBEE BOO
LOVES MOM TOO!

WRITTEN BY:
REENA KORDE PAGNONI

ILLUSTRATED BY:
FRANCES ROSE ESPAÑOL

This is the tale of Rambee Boo,
A kind, sweet dog who's silly too!

Rambee Boo and his brother Rock,
Need to solve a problem with Sock.
They forgot about Mother's Day,
Now it's only a week away.

What can they make that Mom will love?
What special gift, can they think of?
Rock feels anxious, will they have time?
He needs Rambee; his partner in crime.

5 Days Until Mother's Day!

TUESDAY

Rambee wakes with Rock by his side,
Sock is there too, trying to hide.
"Rambee Boo, we have less than a week,
To make a gift that's really unique."

"First thing we'll do on Mother's Day —
Greet Mom with hugs and shout hooray.
We'll shower her with sweet kisses,
And tell her how special she is!"

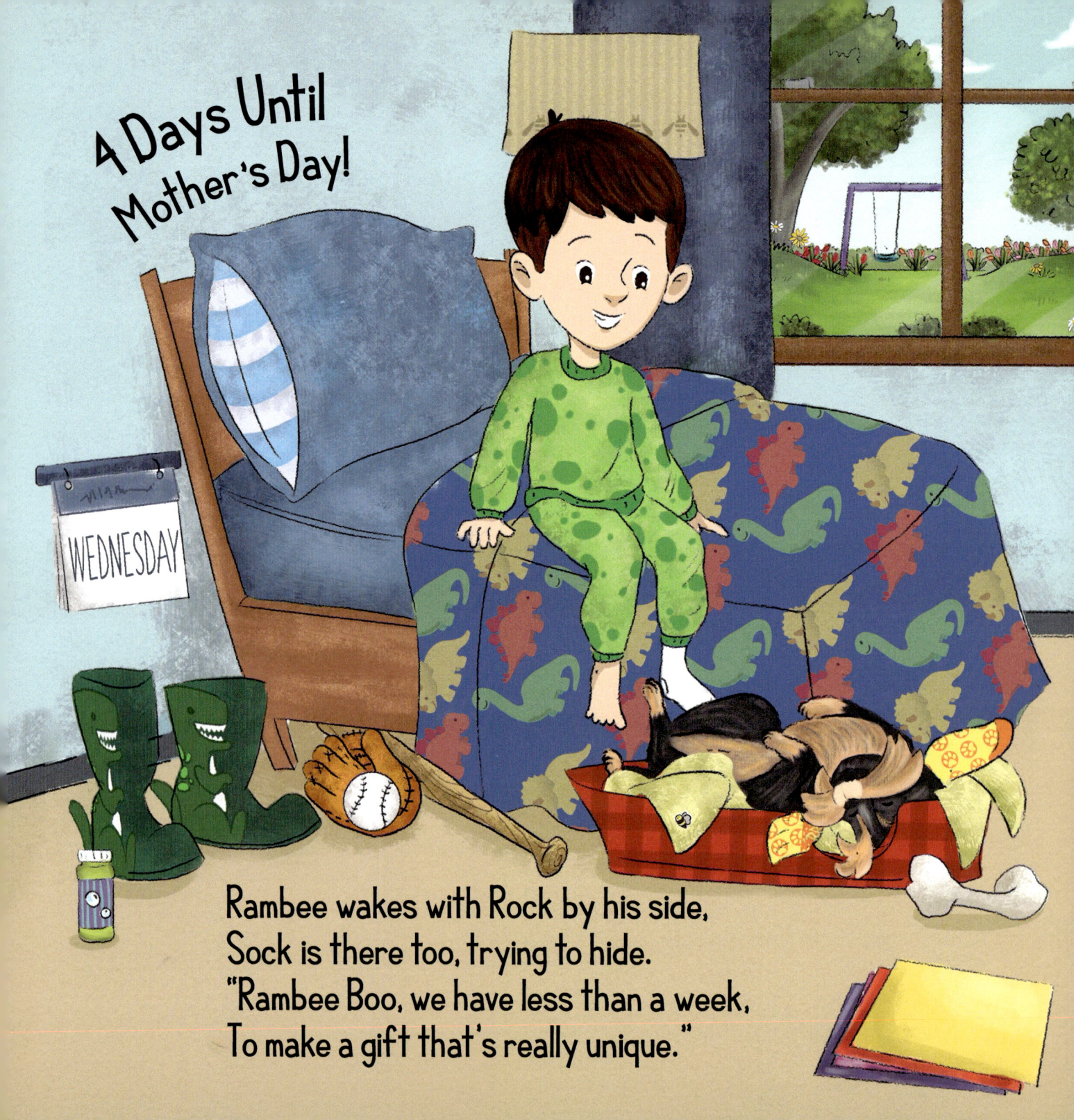

4 Days Until Mother's Day!

WEDNESDAY

Rambee wakes with Rock by his side,
Sock is there too, trying to hide.
"Rambee Boo, we have less than a week,
To make a gift that's really unique."

They'll bake a treat, that's what they'll do,
They both love cake, and Mom does too!
The cake burns, but they ice it well,
It looks perfect so Mom can't tell!

Rock pulls out his bin of supplies.
"What can we make with these?" He cries.
Rambee Boo knows what they can do,
Make a card with glitter and glue.

2 Days Until Mother's Day!

FRIDAY

Rambee wakes with Rock by his side,
Sock is there too, trying to hide.
"Rambee Boo, we have less than a week,
To make a gift that's really unique."

On that day, Rambee Boo and Rock,
Pick some flowers for Mom with Sock.
"Pink tulips will brighten her day."
Rock leads the gang. "C'mon, this way!"

1 Day Until Mother's Day!

SATURDAY

Rambee wakes with Rock by his side,
Sock is there too, trying to hide.
"Rambee Boo, we have less than a week,
To make a gift that's really unique."

Mom would love socks, to warm her toes.
There's just one sock that's loved so close.
They both know, the BEST sock of all,
So, Sock gets wrapped, into a ball!

Mother's Day!

Rambee wakes with Rock by his side,
Sock's still wrapped up as a surprise.
"Wake up, Rambee!" Rock shouts with cheer.
"Mother's Day is finally here!"

Rambee and Rock, with gifts in tow,
Run to Mom's room, they don't tip-toe!

They wake Mom up and shout, "Hooray!"
Hugs and kisses, they make Mom's day.

Mom loves the gifts and all their makes,
She reads the card and eats the cake.
Flowers are in a special place,
Sock puts a big smile on Mom's face.

"I love it, 'cause it's made by you –
Thank you, my Rock and Rambee Boo!"

Happy Mother's Day!

From The Rambee Boo Crew

THE RAMBEE BOO SERIES

RAMBEE BOO WANTS TO KNOW WHAT YOU THINK!

*WHAT ARE SOME THINGS YOU CAN DO TO MAKE MOTHER'S DAY SPECIAL?
*WHAT WAS YOUR FAVORITE GIFT ROCK AND RAMBEE MADE AND WHY?
*WHY DO YOU THINK MOM LOVED SOCK AS A PRESENT?

COLLECTION 1 - COLLECT ALL 6 BOOKS

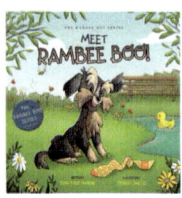 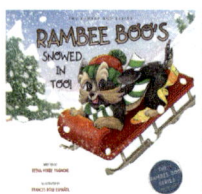    

VISIT WWW.WAMANBOOKS.COM
TAG @THERAMBEEBOOSERIES WITH YOUR FAVORITE RAMBEE BOO BOOK!